Playschool

Helen Oxenbury

WALKER BOOKS
AND SUBSIDIARIES
LONDON • BOSTON • SYDNEY

'Up you get! You mustn't be late
for your first day at playschool.
And you can wear your new shoes.'

'Don't be shy, you'll make
lots of new friends,' Mum said.
'I don't think I'm going to like it,'
I whispered.

'Don't leave me, Mum!'
'It's alright,' the teacher said.
'Your mummy can stay for a bit,
 if you like.'

'This is Nara! She's just hurt her knee.
Look! You've got the same shoes on.'

'I'm just popping out to the shops
for a moment,' said Mum.
'Come on, you two,' the teacher said.
'We can all pretend to be animals.'

The pink teacher read us a story.
We had our elevenses,
and Nara and I shared.

'When you've all been to the lavatory and washed your hands, then we'll sing some songs.'

'Off you go!
Your mums and dads are waiting.
See you all at school tomorrow!'